KURT BUSCH

Kenny Allen

PowerKiDS press™

New York

Published in 2007 by The Rosen Publishing Group, Inc.
29 East 21st Street, New York, NY 10010

Book Design: Michael J. Flynn

Photo Credits: Cover (Busch) © Matthew Stockman/Getty Images; cover (background), pp. 5, 7,
17, 19 © Chris Stanford/Getty Images; p. 9 © Gavin Lawrence/Getty Images; p. 11 © Jonathan
Ferry/Getty Images; p. 13 © Robert Laberge/Allsport; p. 15 © Darrell Ingham/Allsport; p. 21 ©
Streeter Lecka/Getty Images.

Library of Congress Cataloging-in-Publication Data

Allen, Kenny, 1971-
  Kurt Busch / Kenny Allen.
      p. cm. — (NASCAR champions)
  Includes index.
  ISBN-13: 978-1-4042-3457-8
  ISBN-10: 1-4042-3457-8 (lib. bdg.)
  1. Busch, Kurt, 1978—Juvenile literature. 2. Automobile racing drivers—United States—
Biography—Juvenile literature. I. Title. II. Series.
GV1032.B89A27 2007
796.72092—dc22
(B)

                                    2006014308

Manufactured in the United States of America

"NASCAR" is a registered trademark of the National Association for Stock Car Auto Racing, Inc.

Contents

Kurt Busch is a race car driver.
He drives in NASCAR races.

5

Kurt has been racing for a long time. He likes to help fix his own race car.

7

Kurt's brother Kyle is also a race car driver. He races in NASCAR too.

2005

BUDWEISER
PolePower

5 KYLE BUSCH

38.248 | 38.248

Kurt began racing pickup trucks in NASCAR in 2000. He was voted Rookie of the Year.

11

Kurt began racing stock cars full-time in 2001. Stock cars look like the cars people drive on roads.

13

Kurt was the third-best NASCAR driver in 2002. He was only 24 years old!

15

Kurt raced in four all-star races in 2003. He won the all-star championship that year!

RIUS 400

17

Kurt won the NASCAR
championship in 2004.
He was only 26 years old!

18

Kurt had fourteen NASCAR wins by the end of 2005! He is still one of the best drivers in NASCAR.

Glossary

all-star (ALL–STAHR) Made up of people who are the best at a sport.

championship (CHAM-pea-uhn-ship) A contest held to see who is the best in a sport.

pickup truck (PIHK-uhp TRUHK) A small truck that usually has an open bed in the back.

rookie (RU-kee) Someone who is in their first year in a sport.

Books and Web Sites

Books

Buckley, James. *NASCAR.* New York: DK Children, 2005.

Levy, Janey. *Kurt Busch.* New York: Scholastic, 2006.

Web Sites

Due to the changing nature of Internet links, PowerKids Press has developed an online list of Web sites related to the subject of this book. This site is updated regularly. Please use this link to access the list:
http://www.powerkidslinks.com/NASCAR/busch/

Index

A

all-star championship, 16
all-star races, 16

K

Kyle, 8

N

NASCAR championship, 18

P

pickup trucks, 10

R

Rookie of the Year, 10

S

stock cars, 12